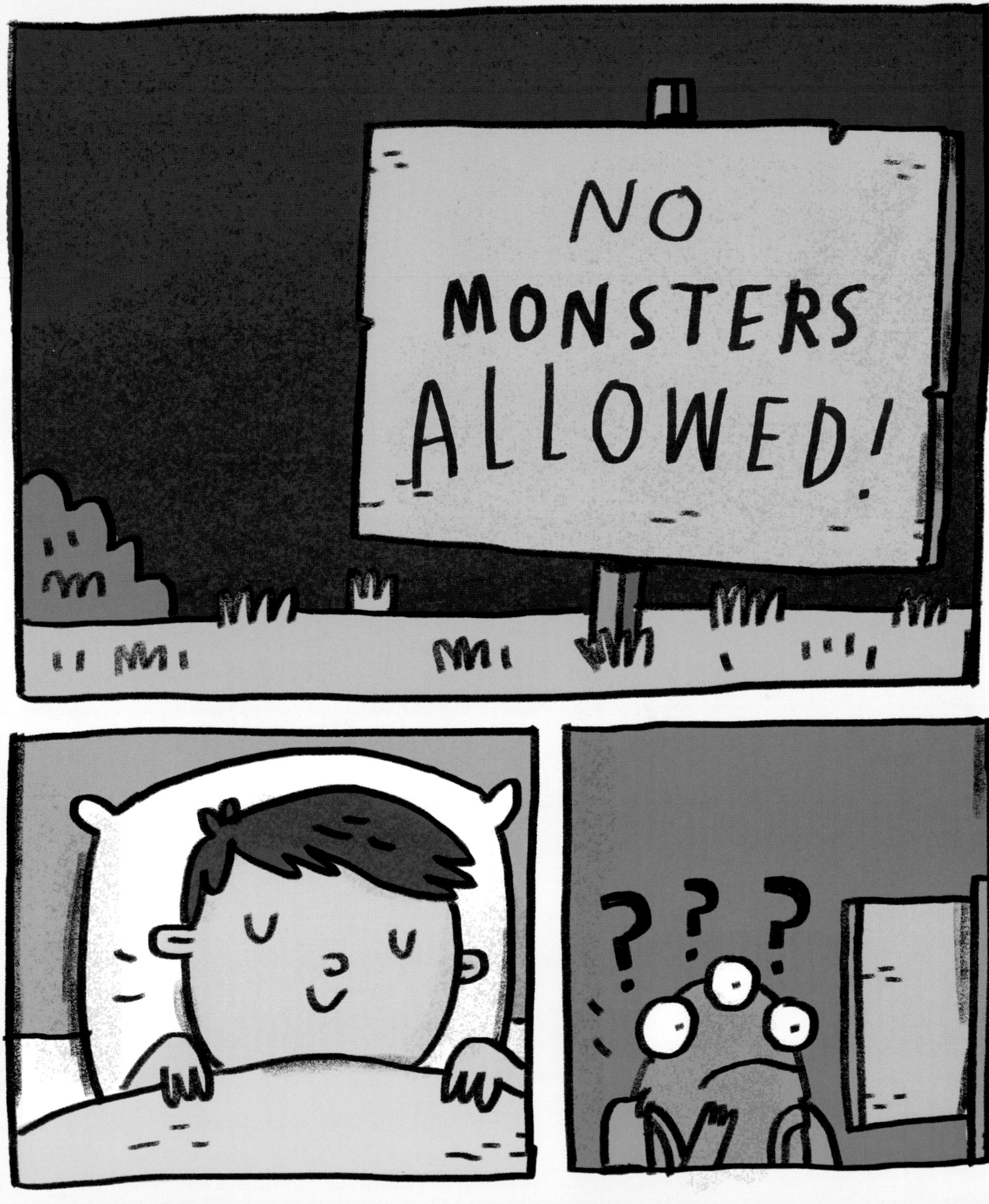
NO MONSTERS ALLOWED!
? ? ?

LATER:

To Beckett, my favorite little monst . . . er . . . boy! ∼L.P.

For my monsters, Allister and Oskar. ∼M.L.

G. P. Putnam's Sons
An imprint of Penguin Random House LLC, New York

Text copyright © 2021 by Lynn Plourde
Illustrations copyright © 2021 by Mike Lowery

Penguin supports copyright. Copyright fuels creativity, encourages diverse voices, promotes free speech, and creates a vibrant culture. Thank you for buying an authorized edition of this book and for complying with copyright laws by not reproducing, scanning, or distributing any part of it in any form without permission. You are supporting writers and allowing Penguin to continue to publish books for every reader.

G. P. Putnam's Sons is a registered trademark of Penguin Random House LLC.

Visit us online at penguinrandomhouse.com

Library of Congress Cataloging-in-Publication Data is available.

Manufactured in China by RR Donnelley Asia Printing Solutions Ltd.
ISBN 9780525515807
1 3 5 7 9 10 8 6 4 2

Design by Marikka Tamura and Suki Boynton
Text set in Fred
The artwork was created using Procreate
on an iPad and finished in Adobe Photoshop.